A. Horsburgh

Sketches in Borneo

A. Horsburgh

Sketches in Borneo

Reprint of the original.

1st Edition 2023 | ISBN: 978-3-37514-790-7

Verlag (Publisher): Salzwasser Verlag GmbH, Zeilweg 44, 60439 Frankfurt, Deutschland
Vertretungsberechtigt (Authorized to represent): E. Roepke, Zeilweg 44, 60439 Frankfurt, Deutschland
Druck (Print): Books on Demand GmbH, In de Tarpen 42, 22848 Norderstedt, Deutschland

SKETCHES IN BORNEO.

BY THE

REV. A. HORSBURGH, A.M.,

LATE MISSIONARY IN SARAWAK,

ANSTRUTHER:
PRINTED BY L. RUSSELL.
MDCCCLVIII.

CHAPTER I.

On the 11th of August 1852, I embarked at Singapore in a small trading schooner bound for Sarawak; and aided by a favourable breeze and a rapid tide, we were soon carried past the verdant shores of the Straits of Malacca, into the China Sea, across which we stretched direct for Borneo. After four days' sail, the outlines of the mountains of that island appeared in the distant horizon, blue and bright through the clear atmosphere, gradually rising up from the water, and darkening in colour, and shewing more clearly their spurs and valleys as we closed in with the land. Next appeared the low level coast-line, black with the forests of centuries, whose dark and heavy verdure stretched in unbroken mass over the whole face of the country, far away over and beyond the tops of the highest and most distant mountains. As we passed along, the coast-line was seen to be occasionally broken by the mouths of large rivers, which discharge their waters through gaps in the ceaseless and apparently impenetrable jungle, and which, by their broad and stately streams, afford access to the interior of the country. We were becalmed for some time off Cape Datu—a high bold promontory that projects far into the sea—till, a heavy squall coming down from the top of the bluff, necessitated a rapid reduction of sail, but bore us at the same time gallantly over the waves. As the night closed in, the clouds gathered in masses; but the almost incessant play of sheet-lightning around the horizon afforded a sufficiency of light by which to continue our course; and about midnight we cast anchor off the Santubong entrance of the Sarawak river.

Next morning the weather was stormy and hazy; but unpropitious as the day was, it gave us a favourable idea of the picturesque character of the country. On one side of the river, close to its mouth, and close also to the beach, Santubong mountain shot up almost perpendicularly to the height of nearly 3000 feet, stretching away seaward in a long, irregular, broken, and picturesque range, and terminating in a bold bluff cape, round whose base the waters of the China Sea heaved and broke. On the other side rose a lower and less striking hill, between which and Santubong the river opened, like the open gate of an avenue, inviting us to explore the country. There we entered with the flood tide, and in due time arrived at Kuching, the capital of the world-famed Sarawak.

I do not intend to repeat the story—so well known through the works of Captains Keppell and Mundy—of the manner in which

Sir James Brooke became Rajah of Sarawak; I may, however, be pardoned giving the following illustration of the cool manner in which he looks danger in the face and prepares against it.

When Mr Brooke first arrived at Kuching in the *Royalist*, he landed and paid his respects to Muda Hassim, the Malay rajah of the place; and in return invited that prince, with several of his nobles and their followers, to visit him on board his yacht. I have shared in the surprise which I have often heard expressed, that Mr Brooke should have invited on board his yacht a Malay prince and his followers, of whom he knew comparatively nothing, except that they belonged to a race whose name is synonymous in the east with ferocity, treachery, and blood-thirstiness, and who, wherever they are known, are noted for their addiction to piracy. It is true, they are by no means so bad as they are represented to be; and it is equally true that they possess many fine qualities, which are discovered upon closer acquaintance; but still the general character they bear, and by which alone Mr Brooke could have known them, is that of treacherous pirates. Mr Brooke, however, resolved to return Muda Hassim's hospitality, without exhibiting either fear or suspicion, while at the same time he took effectual measures to baffle any attempt at treachery, should such be made. On deck, the crew were drawn up under arms, acting ostensibly as a guard of honour to receive the prince, but prepared for hostilities in case of necessity; while at the same time, the ship's guns were loaded with grape, and trained so as to sweep the deck at the first discharge. In the cabin, where Mr Brooke was to receive his visitors, he was seated on a sofa with a broad table placed before him, in order to prevent any sudden stab with a kriss, and under the pillow, which lay carelessly beside him, a pair of loaded pistols were concealed. Above the sofa, a large mirror was placed, and behind the mirror were stationed four men, each with four loaded muskets, who on a given signal were to throw down the mirror, and shew themselves armed. Thus fortified, Mr Brooke sat at his ease, and received his distinguished visitors with gentlemanly courtesy. No attempt at violence was made; and Muda Hassim remained till the day of his death ignorant of the precautions taken against his possible treachery.

On another occasion, after the present Sarawak government was established, a chief of the Sarebas Dyaks, by name Lingire, made an attempt to take Mr Brooke's head. He came to Sarawak with several war-boats, ostensibly to pay a visit to the Malay *Datus* or magistrates of that place, and moored his boats in the river opposite their campongs, a few hundred yards above Rajah Brooke's house. At length, one night when the tide suited his purpose, he dropped silently down the river to the Rajah's wharf, fastened his boats there, and landed with eighty armed men. He then walked up to the house, entered the hall where the Rajah was seated at dinner entertaining all the European inhabitants of the settlement, and his men, placing themselves in a semicircle round the table, squatted down, intending to spring upon their victims in the confusion of clearing away the dinner. As soon as Mr Brooke saw Lingire enter with so many men, he suspected his object, and calling a Malay servant who fortunately understood English, he ordered him to cross the river and tell the Datus to bring over their men as quickly as possible. This being spoken in English, was not understood by the Dyaks, who, thinking that the Rajah had merely given some order about the dinner, saw the servant leave the room without suspicion, and sat still, quietly and intently surveying the scene before them, and waiting the signal of attack from their chief. In the meantime, the Europeans continued their dinner with the best appetite they could, and knowing that their safety depended on their prolonging the meal as much as possible, they were in no hurry to conclude it. From the painful state of suspense in which they were held, they were at length delivered by the arrival of the Datu Tummang-gong—a brave old pirate, who, in his day, has carried on his depredations within sight of Singapore—who entered the room at the head of thirty Malays. He at once placed himself between the Europeans and Dyaks; and turning upon Lingire, he applied to him many epithets the reverse of complimentary, told him that he knew what he had come for, and ordered him instantly to go down to his boats. The Dyak paused; the odds were eighty to thirty, and he seemed inclined to try the chances of a combat; but while he hesitated, the Datu Bandar entered with fifty men, and he then slunk off to his boats like a beaten dog. When he arrived at Sarebas, he gave it out publicly that his object was to have taken the Rajah's head, and he further expressed his determination still to have it; nay, he even went so far as to make a basket for the special purpose of containing it after it should be captured. He now appears, however, to have thought better of the matter; for when I last saw him, he was seated at the Rajah's table, talking and laughing and drinking arrack.

The Sarawak territory, as seen from the sea, presents a long low dark coast-line, covered with trees to the water's edge, and occasionally intersected by the mouths of rivers, or broken by bold rocky promontories that project far into the sea. Behind the coast-line, the ground rises in many places into hills and mountains, some of them round and swelling, and covered, like all the rest of the country, with dark jungle; others abrupt and craggy in the extreme, with trees and bushes shooting from every crevice, and creepers and parasites hanging from every cliff and from every tree.

On entering one of the rivers which cleaves its way through the apparently impenetrable jungle, the traveller finds himself in a wide open channel, both sides of which are crowded with the same dark and heavy foliage that covered the coast, and which, not content with the possession of the land, seems to aspire to that of the water too, by sending forests of mangroves far into the river. In other parts, the banks are lined by thousands of nipa palms, whose long bending leaves, fringed with their dark and sharp-pointed leaflets, wave gracefully in the breeze, forming the foreground of the mighty jungle that towers up behind. Higher up the river, where the banks are no longer swampy, the mangroves and nipas disappear, but the primeval forest still continues in undiminished and unchanging magnificence; and as the silent stream bears us swiftly onwards over its still and placid waters, glowing with the tints of a tropical evening sky, we pass point after point, and traverse reach after reach, each bank and every change of scene presenting the same wild and lonely grandeur and luxuriance. If a pigeon flies overhead, a monkey leaps from a bough, or the loud and discordant note of some feathered denizen of the forest rings through the air, it is the only sign of life the vast jungle exhibits, except the shrill chirping of the tree grasshoppers which have commenced their evening-song, or the irritating attacks which compel attention to the existence of sand-flies and mosquitoes.

As we ascend the river above the influence of the tides, the channel, though it still continues deep, becomes very narrow, and often appears almost over-arched by the vegetation which clothes its banks. Not only do enormous trees shoot up their giant forms to the height of hundreds of feet, but the margin of the river between the trees and the stream itself is lined with a dense mass of vegetation, as thick and impenetrable, and ten times as high, as a quickset-hedge. One of the most remarkable of the plants that form this fringe to the margin of the stream, is called by the Dyaks *mudiang*, and exactly resembles the plant of the pine-apple, only that it grows upon a stem some twenty feet high. Its fruit, also, has much the appearance of the pine-apple, but is hard and woody within, and utterly unfit for food. These plants grow in great numbers in the mud that forms the margin of the stream, and are the resort of troops of monkeys, which leap, grin, and chatter among them during the day, and at night hang asleep upon them within oars-length of the passing boat.

Higher up the river still, it again changes its appearance; instead of being deep and muddy, it becomes shallow and clear, assuming to a considerable extent the character of a mountain stream. The bottom is sandy or stony, and the fish are seen playing in the pools; the banks are dry and free from mud, allowing the large trees of the jungle to spring up from the margin of the stream, and to interlace their gigantic branches high overhead. Then it is that the forest is seen in all its beauty and in all its grandeur. Tall trunks, straight as an arrow, support the unbroken shade of verdure which clings to their boughs, while long and fantastic creepers embrace the vast columns with their tangled net-work, and hang like festoons from one to another. Occasionally, accident may have cleared a considerable space along the banks, leaving one vast tree standing in comparative solitude, and then is seen the monarch of the forest in all his glory. A vast, massive trunk rises straight as a ship's mast, and without a single branch, to the height of some 200 feet; and from the top of this gigantic column diverge the spreading branches, covered with their heavy masses of dark-green foliage, the whole forming as fine an object as the eye can rest on.

Sometimes these large trees are found in inconvenient proximity to the traveller; they fall across the stream, and bar his progress. If the trunk is immersed so deeply as that there are three or four inches of water on any part of it, the canoe is unloaded, and the crew, jumping into the water, drag her over the impediment; while if it happens to be resting at a height of five or six inches above the surface of the stream, she is again unloaded, and pushed underneath it.

As the trees seldom fall perfectly flat across the surface of the water, one or other of these methods of passing them is generally practicable; but sometimes neither of them can be followed, in which case there is no other resource than the laborious and tedious process of cutting the trunk through. As there are also shallows and rapids, as well as logs of wood in the rivers, it will easily be imagined that ascending these smaller streams is a toilsome method of journeying; and so numerous are impediments of one kind or another, that I have sometimes seen the crew wading or swimming continuously for several hours.

I have thus endeavoured to give an idea of the country as seen in going up one of the large rivers. I shall now ask the reader to take a walk with me into the jungle. Jungle is of two kinds—old and young. Old jungle is simply the forest, young jungle is the vegetation which springs up wherever old jungle has been cut down. It consists of a dense mass of grass, reeds, and bushes, impervious to man; and when necessity compels him to take his course through it, he must cut his way with his *parang* or chopping knife, hewing out a path as he goes along. Walking in old jungle, however, is very different. There, there is comparatively little underwood; the ground is moist and soft with decaying leaves; the air is cool and pleasant; and the enormous trees whose foliage completely keeps off the sun, form a 'leafy labyrinth' of the most imposing and extensive dimensions. Every tenth tree is a giant, whose vast stem, straight as a ship's mast, shoots up aloft till its almost undiminished diameter is hid by the foliage of those around it and from the visible height of the lower trees which conceal its top, we are left to imagine the size of the higher. Some of them are covered with the strangest-looking creepers and parasites which clothe the stem and festoon the boughs; and occasionally we come to a tree in full flower, which, if it be partially isolated, so as to admit of its being seen from below, affords one of the most beautiful spectacles which the vegetable creation can present. Altogether, though the general appearance of the forest is, except as regards the size of the trees which compose it, very much like that of a wood at home, still the most cursory examination will not fail to shew something very unlike any of the vegetable productions of the temperate zone. Perhaps, however, one of the most striking features of the jungle is the almost entire absence of animal life which it displays—an absence perfectly surprising to the European visitor, who, from the jungle's being unfrequented and almost untrodden by man, is prepared to find it filled with tenants of one kind or other. But no ; he walks along amidst this luxuriance of vegetation, and scarcely sees an animal. Almost the only signs of life he discovers are the harsh cry of the hornbill, the plaintive wail of the *waua* or long-armed ape, and the loud but melancholy groaning of the *rassong* or long-nosed monkey; or perhaps the sight of a lizard ascending the rough trunk of some vast tree, or a snake rustling among the fallen leaves or twining among the branches. It is true, that where there are many fruit trees, the scene is different ; there troops of monkeys abound, and leap and sport among the boughs, now shaking the forest in very wantonness, again sitting gravely on some lower bough, grinning secure defiance on their two-legged brethren below, treating with majestic contempt the efforts of the Dyaks to frighten them, and gazing with the bliss of ignorance on the terrors of the gun. They are of many hues and of all sizes, from the orang-outang, whose body is as large as that of a tall man, to the smaller species of a span long. There are many birds, too, of different kinds, generally with harsh voices and brilliant plumage, which conceal themselves among the thick leaves, or flit away on too near an approach. Such assemblages of animals, however, are the exception; the rule in the forest is, as I have already stated, great luxuriance of vegetation, and great scarcity of animal life ; and in this respect, Borneo at present, I should imagine, somewhat resembles the account given by geologists of England during the formation of the coal. If it be so, it is strange to find the state of our own island many thousand ages ago paralleled by the present state of another island many thousand miles distant.

There is yet another view of the country which I shall endeavour to present—namely, that witnessed from the summit of a lofty mountain. From such a position, as far as the spectator's eye can reach, he looks down upon a generally flat but somewhat undulating country, with hills of various forms and sizes scattered around, some of them round and swelling, some with sharp peaks and ridges, and some abrupt and craggy in the extreme, but all of them covered with the same dark and heavy verdure which over-spreads the face of the country, except where some limestone cliff gleams through the mass of vegetation which elsewhere shrouds it. In the low ground, he sees the winding rivers pursuing their tortuous course through the unbroken forest, now appearing lustrous and silvery in the light, now red and muddy as they roll along almost at his feet, now buried in the tall trees which clothe their banks, and again reappearing at a distance brighter and more lustrous than ever. The vast expanse of forest spread out before him, induces ideas somewhat akin to those awakened by gazing on the ocean from a sea-side cliff. There is the same extent of prospect, the same monotony of scene, and the same feeling of solitude in the one case as in the other; and this similarity of landscape induces a similarity of ideas, cutting off the soul, as it were, from immediate contact with his fellows, and opening it to the greatness and the majesty of that Power who created alike the ocean and the forest.

CHAPTER II.

THE PEOPLE.

The inhabitants of Sarawak are of three different races—Dyaks, Malays, and Chinese. The Dyaks are the aborigines of the island; the Malays, a sea-faring race who have settled on the coast, and have to a considerable extent compelled the Dyaks to retire inland; and the Chinese are immigrants who have settled in the country, and form a distinct community in the midst of either the Malays or Dyaks, as chance may have placed them. The Malays and Chinese are so well known, that I will say little concerning them, but shall merely reproduce a parallel which I have sometimes mentally drawn between these two races on the one hand, and the Scottish Highlanders and Lowlanders on the other.

The Chinese, like the Lowland Scotch, are cautious, clear-headed, persevering, industrious, and frugal without being niggardly. They lay hold of every opportunity of bettering their circumstances, turn everything to account, and stick all together. They have a keen relish for the humorous, are very hospitable, and excessively proud—proud of themselves and their attainments, proud of their country and its greatness, reckoning themselves the first people, and it the first nation by many degrees on the face of the earth. They emigrate in great numbers to all the countries with which they are acquainted; and though they strive to return to their own land with a competence, they often settle permanently abroad. So far, I think, the characters of the two nations run parallel; but beyond this point the comparison turns into a contrast. The Chinese are utterly unprincipled and mendacious, and thoroughly selfish; and, though many of them know that " honesty is the best policy," it may be safely said that they are never honest from principle.

The Malays, on the other hand, are proud, hot-blooded, and revengeful; expert in the use of arms, fond of war, and unfond of work; fierce and ferocious when excited, but polite and gentlemanly in their ordinary conduct, always civil, and often obliging. They are very fond of their children—so fond, that they never correct them; and the indulgence with which they are treated when young is probably one cause of the high sense of personal dignity which they possess, and why they so deeply feel anything like slight or insult. If they quarrel, they never apply abusive epithets to each other, like Chinese or Hindoos; they are too proud to scold, and their resentment is too deep to be vented in words. They are not exactly brave, in our sense of the word; that is, they have not the cool calm courage of western nations, at least of disciplined men; but when their blood is roused, they lose all regard for personal consequences, and fight like furies to the death. "You must surely give your men something to inspire courage," said a Malay who witnessed Keppell's attack on Patusan to one of the Europeans, "for they rush up right in face of the cannons. Now we Malays are brave, but we cannot do that." Yet this man bears a high character for courage, and was the first to scale the enemy's palisade at Sunge Lang (Kite's River), preceding even Europeans in the attack.

The Dyaks are a branch of the Malay race, and differ little from the ordinary Malay type. They have broad faces, flat noses, thickish lips, black eyes, and coarse lank black hair. They are fairer than the Malays, some of them when young being as fair as a European; but as they grow up and expose themselves to the sun, they become of a reddish brown, like the savages of the Amazon, whom, I have been told, they much resemble in many respects. They are smaller, and possess less physical strength than Europeans, but they have great powers of endurance, and great bodily activity, climbing rocks and trees like cats or monkeys Their countenance is, as I have said, of the Malay type, and it consequently takes some time before a European becomes accustomed to their appearance; but when his eye has been reconciled to their cast of features, he soon discovers in them intelligence, openness, sprightliness, and good-humour. These qualities never fail to commend themselves to the favourable consideration of the spectator, and he soon begins to consider them handsome, according as they approach the ideal of the Malay type, just as he considers a European handsome, according as he approaches the ideal of the Caucasian type. The ordinary dress of the men consists of a *chawat*, or piece of cloth, about six inches wide, and six or eight feet long, passed once between the legs, and wrapped several times round the waist, one end of it hanging down in front, the other behind. They also wear a jacket of thick cotton cloth of their own manufacture, and a handkerchief or piece of bark-cloth tied like a turban around the head. The women wear a petticoat of much scantier dimensions than a Highlander's kilt, together with a jacket like that of the men. Few of either sex, however, wear the jacket, except in cold weather; the men, if on a journey, generally carrying theirs in a basket, while the women hang theirs over one shoulder. Many men wear their hair long like the women, but most of them wear it short, while a few shave the head completely bare. Both sexes are fond of adorning their hair or head-dresses with flowers, generally large bright red and yellow blossoms, which become their dark complexions exceedingly well.

Of *national* ornaments, as they may be called, there are no great variety, and most of them, though still retained by the inland tribes, are being abandoned by those who have come much in contact with Europeans. The most striking to the eye of a stranger are the large and numerous ear-rings worn by the tribes of Sarebas and Sakarran, and which are inserted not only in the lobe, but also in the cartilage of the ear. Five or six large brass rings—the largest being sometimes four inches in diameter—are suspended in the lobe of the ear, and eight or ten more, in regularly diminishing order as they ascend, are inserted in the cartilage. The women do not wear these enormous ear-rings, their peculiar ornament being a circlet of painted rattan hoops around the waist. Both sexes wear numerous bracelets and anklets of brass-wire, and frequently also armlets of polished white shell, which contrast well with their dusky forms. On one occasion, I saw the daughters of several Sakarran chiefs clothed in loose dresses composed of shells, beads, and polished stones, arranged with great care and considerable taste. The dress, which was very becoming, hung as low as the knee, and as the young ladies walked along, the stones of which it was composed rung upon each other like the chime of distant bells. These dresses are very expensive, costing some seventy or eighty reals a-piece (about £12), and are therefore not common.

Some of the young men wear head-dresses composed of the hair of their enemies, dyed red, with which they also ornament the heads of their spears and the handles and scabbards of their swords. Others adorn themselves with the feathers of the argus pheasant, and many with fantastic artificial plumes. At Sampro, I saw a woman wearing a long round hat, somewhat resembling the head-dress of a Parsee, but narrower, and much more lofty. The Malos and Kyans tattoo themselves slightly, and generally each tribe has some trifling distinction in dress or ornament peculiar to themselves.

In disposition, the Dyaks are mild and gentle; they are quiet and docile when well treated, but proud and apt to take offence if they think themselves slighted. They are industrious, frugal, and accumulative, and, were they not so poor, might even be reckoned stingy; but as each knows that, if from the failure of his crop, or from any other unavoidable cause, he should fall into debt, it will accumulate so rapidly, from the high rate of interest, that he will probably never get free from it, the carefulness and frugality which they display cannot be regarded as otherwise than legitimate. At the same time, they are hospitable to the extent of their means, and consider themselves bound to place before a visitor the best they can afford. They have a strong perception of the distinction between *meum* and *tuum*, and scarcely ever violate it either among themselves or towards Europeans. They never attempt such thefts and robberies as the South Sea islanders were in the habit of committing upon the early navigators; for their great self-esteem, their high sense of personal and family dignity, and the intense keenness with which they feel anything like degradation, would alone prevent their doing anything to which infamy was attached. As they are thus honest, so are they to a great extent truthful, though to this general character there are, of course, exceptions. On one occasion, a Dyak said to a missionary:—"Your religion is for sinners, is it not?" "Yes," he replied, "it is for all men to teach them to be good, and to do God's will." "Very well," was the answer; "you should try and convert that man," pointing to one who passed by, "for he is a thief." But though the Dyaks do not steal, they are great beggars; for they have been so accustomed to receive things from white men, that they think they have only to ask for anything they may want. Their pride, however, is so great, that a few rebuffs effectually check them; and they have, besides, a delicacy of feeling, and an innate sense of the becoming, which prevent their doing anything improper or contrary to natural good manners. When they receive a present, they never say "Thank you," but next day they will bring in return a little fruit or some such trifle: it is their method of making an acknowledgement.

When young, the Dyaks are acute and apt to learn, but as they grow older, their intellect seems to become deadened, and incapable of rising beyond familiar subjects. The cause of this seems to be, that having neither religion nor poetry, having nothing that can elevate the mind above the routine of ordinary life, or cause the past, the distant, or the future to predominate over the present, their faculties are bowed down to the daily wants of their daily existence, and become incapable of expanding beyond them. I have observed that those lads who are in the habit of associating with the missionaries, and have been by them instructed in Christianity, are much more acute and intelligent than their companions; and I think it not unlikely that they may retain through life that mental superiority which they now unquestionably possess. Let us hope, then, that Christianity, which has done so much for every other nation by whom it has been received, will do as much for them, and that they will be elevated both morally and intellectually by being taught the sublime and affecting narrative of the Saviour's life and death.

There are in the Sarawak territory many different tribes of Dyaks, named from the rivers on which they live, many of them speaking distinct languages, and almost all of them habitually regarding each other as enemies. These tribes, prior to the coming of Sir James Brooke, lived in a state of chronic hostility with each other. Whenever they met, they fought. They either fitted out numerous fleets to combat on a large scale, or they went out in small parties of one or two boats, stealing upon their enemies by surprise, and retreating as suddenly as they came. The object of all these expeditions was to procure human heads. The head of an enemy is the most valued prize a Dyak can have, and is not only esteemed as a trophy of valour, but is also intimately connected with their superstitious customs. The death of one of their tribe entailed an *ulat* or ban upon the whole country; and until this ulat was removed, which it only could be by the capture of a head, various restrictions were placed upon the whole community—for example, no widower could marry again, nor could the appropriate offerings at the tombs of their deceased relatives be made till the ulat was removed. There were, therefore, many excuses for head-hunting. If the near relative of a chief died, he immediately organised a head-hunting expedition, viewing the heads captured probably, though now unconsciously, as an offering to the *manes* of the deceased. At other times, they went out to avenge former attacks by hostile tribes, and often again, merely for the love of war and the glory of taking heads. Nor were they at all particular whose head they took. Primarily, of course, their expeditions were directed against enemies; but with them, every stranger was an enemy; and a disappointed war-party would sooner take the head of a friend, than return without one. Thus head-hunting became with them a passion, and in its palmy days, before it was so much put down by Sir James Brooke, a young man could scarcely get married before he had taken a head. If they fitted out a large fleet of war-boats, they would swiftly and silently approach a village, surround it at night, or rather just before morning, set fire to the houses, and massacre indiscriminately men, women, and children, and then depart in triumph with their heads; or if a small war-party of six or seven men embarked in a fast boat, they would conceal it in the umbrageous creeks near an enemy's house, and then prowling about in the jungle, would pounce upon any unfortunate who might stray near them. Sometimes they would even get into the wells of their enemies, and, covering their heads with a few leaves, sit for hours in the water waiting for a victim. Then when any woman or girl came to draw water, they would rush out upon her, cut her down, take her head, and flee into the jungle with it before any alarm could be given. Sometimes a war-party would decoy a party of traders, and murder them for the sake of their heads; while a trading-party, if opportunity offered, never failed to act in a similar manner. Thus no party of Dyaks was ever safe from any other party : they lived, as I said before, in a state of chronic hostility with all their neighbours, attacking and being attacked by all around them.

This was the general state of Dyak society before the coming of Sir James Brooke; but there are two tribes who, from the atrocities they perpetrated, from the extent of country they devastated, and from the attacks to which Sir James Brooke was subjected, for having broken their power, merit a peculiar notice. These are the Dyaks of Sarebas and Sakarran.

These tribes were more numerous, more powerful, and better organised for purposes of aggression than any of the others, being to a considerable extent under the authority of Malay chiefs, who employed the head-hunting propensities of the Dyaks to further their own piratical inclinations. They would call out a fleet of 100 or 200 war-boats—each containing on an average about thirty-five men—and with this formidable force they would plunder and devastate the whole coast from Pontianak to Barram, a distance of 400 miles. Villages were surrounded and whole tribes cut off. Many communities were broken up, and their families forced to flee, some to more powerful tribes, others to remote fastnesses and distant countries. Men at their fishing-stakes, and women and children in their rice-fields, were surprised and murdered, and the country was fast becoming depopulated and desert. These fleets were led by the Malays, who appropriated the plunder that was captured, while the Dyaks received what they prized most—the heads. Of these bloody trophies, great numbers were taken, sometimes as many as 400 in a single expedition. Nor did they confine their attacks to other Dyaks against whom it might be supposed they had cause of war: they fell upon all who had plunder either to gratify the Malays, or heads to satisfy themselves. All whom they met they attacked, Dyaks, Malays, Chinese, and Europeans; villages ashore, or vessels afloat, all were equally subject to their indiscriminate ravages. To put a stop to these ravages, and to break their aggressive power, was the first step towards the pacification of the country; a step as absolutely indispensable as would be the destruction of a den of tigers in the vicinity of an Indian village. No other tribe could cultivate the arts of peace, or do anything else than prepare for war, when liable to be attacked any day or night by the men of Sarebas and Sakarran.

Such were the tribes whom Sir James Brooke attacked, and whose power he broke; and it was on account of the severe chastisement which he inflicted upon them that he was branded in this country as a mercenary and bloodthirsty murderer. Fortunately for the interests of humanity he was not deterred by the attacks made upon him from pursuing the line of conduct he had marked out for himself; but after having effectually broken the aggressive power of the Dyaks, he took measures to pacify the country and to give security to life and property. This he has succeeded to a great extent in doing, and the consequences have been most gratifying, and almost wonderful. The late outbreak of the Chinese has of course given a shock to the prosperity of the settlement, and probably thrown it back about three years ; but I am sure it will not really injure it, though I can only speak of the country as I saw it previous to that event. At that period, people from neighbouring districts had flocked, and were flocking, into Sir James's territory to enjoy the benefits of his government; the resources of the country were being rapidly developed ; trade had increased, and was increasing, to an astonishing extent ; tribes of savages whose only delight was in bloodshed, and who regarded the possession of a human head as the *summum bonum*, have to a great extent been turned from their bloody courses, and taught to devote their superfluous energies to the increased production of the fruits of the earth. Larger breadths of land are being brought into cultivation, yet all the crops are consumed in the country, and it is necessary often to import rice for the increasing population. Pepper and gambier, and many other crops, are being introduced ; sago is largely produced and manufactured; mines are wrought, and smelting establishments erected ; gold is found in tolerable quantities, and antimony, and, above all, coal will soon be wrought on a large scale. In short, Sarawak has become the emporium of trade and the centre of civilisation to the whole north-west coast of Borneo, and so far as man can presume to look into the future, Sir James Brooke seems there to have laid the foundation of a great, and, let us hope, a durable and a Christian empire. This has he done, and thus has he earned for himself a place in the noble list of the benefactors of mankind, while in the government of his principality he has displayed a tact and an ability that have extorted the commendation even of his enemies. He is one of her sons of whom England may well be proud, one who in his lesser sphere has exhibited a courage and a capacity akin to that displayed by the founders and restorers of our Indian Empire.

CHAPTER III.

SOCIAL LIFE.

The Dyaks live in communities of from ten or twenty to forty families, all of them residing in one house under the headship of one *Tuah*, or elder, whose influence among them depends very much on his personal qualifications. If he is brave and otherwise popular he will have many followers, and will be able to exercise great authority over them ; but if, from any cause, he makes himself unpopular, he will be deserted by all his adherents, and from being a Chief he will sink down to the condition of a common man. The house in which each community lives, is an edifice of from fifty to a hundred yards in length, and raised on posts eight or ten feet high. Its framework is constructed of posts lashed together with split rattans; while the roof and partitions are composed of *attaps*, a kind of thatch, so simple and useful as to merit a distinct description. It is made of the leaves of the Nipa, a palm which grows in the mud on the banks of the rivers, and differs from most other palms in having no trunk, being merely a collection of fronds proceeding from one root. Each frond consists of a stem or midrib, about twenty or thirty feet in length, on each side of which grow a series of leaves, two or three feet long, and two or three inches broad. To form attaps, the Dyaks cut off these leaves, and double them over a stick a yard long, making them overlap each other, so as to be impervious to rain. They then sew or interlace them all firmly with split rattans; thus forming a sort of leaf-tile, at once strong and light, and well adapted for excluding both sun and rain. The house is divided longitudinally in the middle by a partition, on one side of which is a series of rooms, and on the other a kind of gallery or hall upon which the rooms open. In these rooms, each of which is inhabited by a distinct family, the married couples and children sleep ; the young unmarried women sleep in an apartment over the room of their parents, and the young men in the gallery outside. In this gallery likewise, which serves as a common hall, their principal occupations are carried on, the planks of their war-boats, their large mats, and all their more bulky articles are kept, and the grim trophies of their wars, the scorched and blackened heads of their enemies, are suspended in bundles.* The floor is a kind of spar-work, composed of split palm-trunks, and raised ten or twelve feet from the ground, access being given to it by a ladder, or more frequently by a log of wood cut into the form of steps. Connected with the gallery, and running along the whole length of the house, there is a broad platform on the same level as the floor, upon which the Dyaks spread out their rice after harvest, and expose such other articles as they wish to be dried in the sun.

Thus, a Dyak house is rather a singular structure ; and when imbosomed, as it often is, among cocoa-nut, plantain, and other fruit-trees, forms a quietly pleasing and picturesque object, suggestive of much social happiness enjoyed in a simple state of society. It awakens, moreover, ideas of a higher kind, for it is a sign of the presence of all subduing man on the confines of the jungle that is yet to fall before his axe.

The materials of which these edifices are constructed are so fra-

*Among the Sarawak Dyaks the skulls are not suspended in the house in which the community lives, but in a small separate house erected for the purpose, called the head-house, and which likewise serves as a caravansera for the reception of strangers.

gile that they require to be rebuilt every five or six years, and when this necessity occurs, the Dyaks, instead of erecting the new house in the immediate vicinity of the old one, generally remove to a considerable distance. Thus they place themselves in the midst of a new country in which to recommence their farming operations, and are thus probably the most nomadic of all the races of men who devote themselves to agriculture.

From the above description, it will be seen that a Dyak house may with more propriety be called a village, as it is the residence of about a score of families who live in a series of rooms under one roof, and all of whom look up to one Tuah, or Elder, as their head. These house are sometimes in groups of two or three, but more frequently they stand alone ; and thus it happens that if the tribe is populous, it may be scattered over a very great extent of country.

Besides the Tuahs, there is another and superior class of chiefs called *Orang Kaya* (rich men), grave steady old men of good family, who, when young, have distinguished themselves by their courage ; and who, in their riper years, are regarded as discreet judges in weighty matters of the law. Even the power of an Orang Kaya, however, is extremely limited. He has no actual authority over his followers, so as to compel them to do anything against their will ; his superiority is shown only in leading them to battle, and acting as a judge in conjunction with other chiefs. In other respects, the chiefs are scarcely to be distinguished from other Dyaks. They work at their farms and their boats as hard as their own slaves ; they wear the same dress, and live in the same manner as the rest of the community ; their only token of chieftainship being the respect which is voluntarily accorded to their personal qualities, and the deference which, in matters of deliberation, is paid to their opinion. To an assembly of chiefs, all disputes are referred, and their decisions are given in accordance with their own customs, which, besides guiding the verdict, generally settle the penalty which shall be inflicted on the aggressor. Cases which, from want of evidence or from uncertainty of any kind, cannot be thus decided, are settled by an appeal to superior powers in an ordeal by diving.

When both parties in a dispute have agreed that it should be referred to the diving ordeal, preliminary meetings are held to determine the time, place, and circumstances of the match. On the evening of the day previous to that on which it is to be decided, each party stakes in the following manner a certain amount of property, which, in case of defeat, shall come into the possession of the victor. The various articles of the stake are brought out of the litigant's room, placed in the verandah of the house in which he lives, and are there covered up and secured. One man who acts as a kind of herald then rises, and in a long speech, asks the litigant whether he is conscious he is in the right, and trusts in the justice of his cause ; to which the latter replies at equal length in the affirmative, and refers the matter to the decision of the spirits. Several more speeches and replies follow; and the ceremony concludes by an invocation of justice upon the side of right. In the meantime, the respondent deposits and secures his stake with like ceremonial in the verandah of his own house; and early in the morning, both parties, accompanied by their respective friends, repair to the bank of the river to decide the contest. Either party may appear by deputy, a privilege which is always taken advantage of by women, and often even by men, for there are many professional divers who, for a trifling sum, are willing to undergo the stifling contest. Preparations are now made; the articles staked are brought down and placed on the bank; each party lights a fire, at which to recover their champion, should he be nearly drowned; and each provides a roughly constructed grating for him to stand on, and a pole to be thrust into the mud for him to hold on by. The gratings are then placed in the river within a few yards of each other, where the water is deep enough to reach to the middle; the poles are thrust firmly into the mud; and the champions, each on his own grating grasping his pole, and surrounded by his friends, plunge their heads simultaneously under water. Immediately the spectators chant aloud at the top of their voices the mystic, and perhaps once intelligible word *lobōn-lobōn*, which they continue repeating during the whole contest. When at length one of the champions shews signs of yielding, his friends, with the laudable desire of preventing his being beaten, hold his head forcibly under water. The excitement is now great; *lobōn-lobōn* increases in intensity, and redoubles in rapidity; the shouts become yells, and the struggles of the unhappy victim, who is fast becoming asphyxied, are painful to witness. At length, nature can endure no more: he drops senseless in the water, and is dragged ashore, apparently lifeless, by his companions; while the friends of his opponent, raising one loud and prolonged note of triumph, hurry to the bank, and seize and carry off the stakes. All this, however, is unknown to the unhappy vanquished, who, pallid and senseless, hangs in the arms of his friends, by whom his face is plastered with mud, in order to restore animation. In a few minutes, in spite rather than in consequence of this treatment, respiration returns; he opens his eyes, gazes wildly around, and in a short time is perhaps able to walk home. Next day, he is in a high state of fever, and has all the other symptoms of a man recovering from apparent death by drowning.

This manner of settling disputes is well suited to the Dyaks, for it affords a method of deciding matters regarding which there is no evidence, and on which there would be no other mode of coming to a conclusion. The result of the trial, whatever it be, is regarded as the verdict of a higher power, and is never questioned. Even in cases where the loser knows he is right—when, for example, a man is unjustly accused of theft, and conscious of innocence, appeals to the ordeal, and loses his cause—he never thinks of blaming the decision, but attributes his defeat to some previous sin, for which the superior powers are now inflicting punishment.

I may here mention a method of divination employed by the Malos, or tinkers, of Borneo, a race who, from their skill in working metals, travel and are welcomed almost everywhere, and by whom —for they are the most superstitious race with whom we have come in contact—are told stories wild as any in the *Arabian Nights*. In a case of theft which happened at Banting, suspicion was divided among three persons, and the principal Malo man of the place, by name Ramba, undertook to discover which of them was the culprit. For this purpose he took three bamboos, partially filled with water, and, assigning one to each of the suspected persons, arranged them round a fire with mystic rites and barbaric spells, in the full belief that the bamboo assigned to the culprit would be the first to eject a portion of its contents by ebullition. One of them at length did so, and it so happened that it was the bamboo assigned to him against whom the little evidence that could be collected bore hardest. Shortly afterwards, another also boiled over, while the third would not do so at all. The possessor of the first was accordingly declared by Ramba to be the culprit, while the possessor of the last was declared to be certainly innocent. Fortunately for the credit of the Dyaks, they would not act upon the information thus obtained; and unfortunately for the credit of the diviner, it was afterwards discovered that he whose bamboo would not boil over at all was the thief.

Next to the chiefs, the most important class among the Dyaks are the Mannangs, who combine the functions of doctor and priest, and who are in great request in all cases of public or private calamity or rejoicing. They are of both sexes, some of the males being dressed as women—an innocent relic of some forgotten custom. Mannangs marry and work at their boats, houses, and farms, in all respects like other Dyaks, from whom they would be undistinguishable, but for their appearance on public or important private occasions. They are paid for their services by those who employ them, and their ranks are recruited by young men who desire to enter the order, and who, with various ceremonies, are admitted into the fraternity. Many of these young men are blind, and depend upon their profession for their subsistence, while others are flattered by that consideration which intercourse with the spirits gives them among their fellows. Mannangs, however, are not held in much respect; they are looked upon in a great measure as a set of pretenders, whose principal object is to extract money from those who employ them; and are regarded as the degenerate descendants of a former race of powerful ghost-expellers, soul-compellers, prophets, priests, clairvoyants, and healers of bodily ailments, whose mantles have not fallen upon their successors. Still they are much employed

c

for the human mind, and cannot do without religion, or at least some substitute for it.

I cannot from my own knowledge describe the manner of making a Manuang, as I purposely avoided witnessing it, but I believe the ceremony to be as follows :—A number of Manuangs assemble at the house of the candidate's father, and seating themselves in a circle, with the candidate in the centre, one of them begins a low monotonous and dreary chant, which the rest at stated intervals take up, joining in a sort of chorus. This chant, which consists of an irregularly alliterated versification, with little or no meaning, is uttered in a monotonous and dismal tone, to which it is most dreary and irritating to be compelled to listen. This portion of the ceremony takes place in the presence of a large number of spectators, who on its conclusion are excluded from the room, and the subsequent initiatory rites are performed in private. The door is shut, the apartment is darkened, and a solemn silence prevails; a fowl is sacrificed, and its blood sprinkled around the room. The head of the candidate is split open with a sword, in order that his brain may be cleansed from that obtuseness which, in the generality of mankind, precludes the knowledge of future events. Gold is placed in his eyes, to enable him to see the spirits; hooks are inserted into his fingers, to enable him to extract, from the bodies of the sick, fish-bones, stones, and other foreign substances; and his senses generally are in like manner supernaturally strengthened. He then emerges a perfect Manuang; and in order to complete his education, requires only to be taught the tricks and chants of the brotherhood.

Though the Dyaks believe in the existence of superior powers, and perhaps in One who is supreme over all the rest, they have no very consistent mythology. The following account of the creation is given by the Dyaks of Sakarran :—

In the beginning, existed in solitude, Rajah Gantallah, possessed of a soul with organs for hearing, speaking, and seeing; but destitute of any other limbs or members: he rested upon a *lumbu*. *Lembu* is the Malay word for a bull or cow; but it was not upon this animal he had his seat; nor were the Dyaks able to give any account of what a lumbu is. By an act of his will, Rajah Gantallah originated two birds, a male and a female, after which he did not directly produce any creature, his will taking effect through the instrumentality of these birds. They dwelt on the lumbu, above, beneath, and around, in what was originally a void. Whilst dwelling upon it, they created first the sky, then the earth, and then the Batang Lupar—a large river in Borneo—which was the first of waters, and the mother of rivers. Leaving the lumbu, they flew round the earth and sky, to discover which of them was the greater. Finding that the size of the earth considerably exceeded that of the sky, they collected the earth together with their feet, and heaped it into mountains. Having completed this work, they attempted to create mankind. For this end, they made the trees, and tried to turn them into men; but without success. They then made the rocks for the same purpose. These they shaped liked a man in all respects; but the figure was destitute of the power of speech. They then took earth, and, by the aid of water, moulded it into the form of a man, infusing into his veins the gum of the kumpang-tree, which is of a red colour. They called to him—he answered; they cut at him—blood flowed from his wounds; as the day waxed hot, sweat oozed through his skin. They gave him the name of Tannah Kumpok, or Moulded Earth.

Besides this account of the creation of the first man, the Dyaks have likewise several traditions regarding the Deluge, one of which, curiously enough, connects it with the universally diffused story of the dragon, the woman, and the fruit of a tree for which she longed.

The following is the narrative as given by the Dyaks of Sakarran :—

"There was a woman, who longed for the fruit of the 'assam paiah.' She ordered her husband to procure it. He went into the jungle for the purpose; but when he arrived at the assam tree, he found it enfolded by a dragon. He returned to his wife, and informed her of the cause of his bringing back none of the fruit. She went herself, and asked the dragon, who uncoiled himself that she might approach the tree. For two or three succeeding days she thus came and ate of the fruit. Soon after a child was born to her; and a few days afterwards, she went to bathe in the Sakarran, taking her child with her. The spot is called to this day, 'The Dragon's Bight.' Having laid her child on the bank, she entered the water. The dragon approached and seized the child. She ran screaming to her house and aroused her neighbours. They set forth to overtake the dragon. After having found in succession seven young dragons, they discovered the lost child dead. They killed the young dragons and took them to their homes, where they prepared to cook them. In one of the pans filled with their flesh, when the water boiled, the boiling made the following intelligible sounds :—

'Gurok gurok, drowned be the bights.

'Gurok gurok, drowned be the headlands.

'Gurit gurit, drowned be the hills.'

Hereupon followed a storm of rain, with thunder, which continued for three days and three nights. During this, the waters rose until they overwhelmed all beneath the sky, excepting some of the mountain tops. To these a few beasts of each kind escaped, and thus survived the flood. The greater portion of mankind was drowned; some, however, fled to the mountains, and others were saved in ships. The former became Dyaks, the latter Malays."

The Malays report other Dyak traditions of this flood; one, if rightly narrated, more closely agrees with the Scriptural narrative of the Deluge.

The following mythology, as given by another party of Dyaks, was read over to Orang kaya Linggi, from whose mouth the preceding narrative was taken down. His comments are added :—

The highest and eldest of the Gods is Bri Kunchan. His dwelling-place is in the waters, and he is ordinarily known by the title of Rajah Boiya, or King of Alligators. To him all birds, men, and gods are subject.

The deity next in order is Singallong-Burong, who dwells at Panjong-Sanang-Sinjong, in the heavens.

After him follows Kling Benowing. To these three the name Batara is confined. They form the same Batara. But by that name in ordinary use is meant this Kling, the especial ruler of birds and men. It is he who helps us all. He is believed to haunt the hill tops. His especial country lies near to the brave, wherever they be, and it is visited by them, perhaps by three out of ten thousand Dyaks. It is Dream-land. It is when men sleep in the woods that they may chance in their dreams to meet with Kling. If on awaking they should speak of having done so, they immediately die or become mad. If they are silent on the subject, great good fortune follows them in consequence of this meeting ; they become brave, rich, and powerful. Gassing and Bulan, of the Sakarran chiefs, and Buah-Riya and Rabboug, of the Kanowit, have met with Kling. Not that themselves have mentioned it ; but this is the universal belief, in consequence of their career.

It is not known who made the earth, sun, or stars. All trees, fruits, and so forth, are the productions of Demong-Penuliong. He is not Batara himself, but is a follower of the before-mentioned Singallong-Burong. Slumpandei is the creator of men. Pulongganah causes the growth of paddi, and gives its increase. He is an independent king. The other kings, named by us "hantus," or spirits—but not the ghosts of men—are not called Batara, but are obedient to him.

In these two statements is an evident contradiction in the application of the term Batara, "from *avatara*—a name adopted from the Hindu system, and applied to various mythological personages." (Marsden.)* A Malay Scriff, dissuading from the use of it to express the word God in their language, declares that the Dyaks apply it " to hantus, birds of omen, and charms, as the spittle of white men when strangers, and so forth." Perhaps the remark of a Dyak chief, who had been present on the previous evening during the narrative of Linggi, may throw some light on the use of the term. He said—"There is but one Being who truly owns the name

---

*The true derivation seems to be the Sanscrit "bhattara"—worthy of veneration. Hardwick's Christ and other Masters, Part III., page 173.

Batara; others are called by it, since they are the eyes, the
Viceroys, or ministers of him."[*]

The Dyaks believe in the existence of a future state in which
a distinction shall be made between good men and bad, but what
that distinction shall be does not seem to be very well known.
The locality of the unseen world—which they term Sebaian—is
placed by them beneath the earth, and it is divided into two
regions—that of the living or Sebaian hidop, and that of the dead
or Sebaian mati. Sebaian hidop is a delightful country, with rich
soil and luxuriant crops. The stalks of tobacco are as thick as a
man's arm; the heads of Indian corn are as big as a man's leg, and
all its other produce is gigantic in proportion. It has human inhabitants concerning whom nothing definite is known, and it is
likewise the abode of an immense number of *hantus* or spirits.
Sebaian mati is the abode of the dead, and like the Homeric Hades,
is a gloomy, desolate, and unlovable region. Here the souls of the
departed wander for a certain time—shorter or longer as they are
good or bad—and at length they pass into the region of the air,
where they are dissolved into dew and precipitated to the earth.[†]

In the opinion above stated there seems to be a trace of the
Bhuddist doctrine of the absorption of the soul into the Deity, and
its consequent annihilation as a distinct existence. I have likewise found among the Dyaks a trace of the doctrine of Metempsy-
chosis. On one occasion, when walking in company with two
Dyak boys, Kassa and Biju, Kassa told me that his grandfather had
become a Prince among the miases or orang-outangs, and that one day
Biju spied this mias in a tree, and not knowing that it had formerly
been a man, threw a stick at it and tried to frighten it. The mias,
indignant at such an insult, exerted its hidden and malignant
influence and smote the offender with a severe fever, from which
with difficulty he recovered. On asking Biju if such were the case,
he admitted the truth of the story, adding such details as left no
doubt that he had once thrown a stick at a mias, and had had a
severe fever after doing so. "But how did you know it was your
grandfather, Kassa?" I asked. With undoubting faith, grave
earnest countenance, and large bright eye, he answered, "Oh, Sir,
most certainly it was!" What logic could stand against this?

I afterwards found upon inquiry, that many Dyaks after death
are supposed to become princes among the miases, and it is further
said that many of these hantu or spirit miases assume the form of
men for purposes of deception. There are several other hantu
beasts, as they may be called—animals which are looked upon with
superstitious feelings, and are supposed to possess semi-supernatural
power.

* S. P. G. F. Quarterly Paper. No. LXXX. January 1854. Missionary
Series.

† Here also they describe one hill covered with the poisonous tuba tree, where
are again united maidens and their lovers who have committed suicide.

The Dyaks distinguish between the soul—which they term *semungat*—and the animal life. In cases of severe sickness they say that the soul has left the body, has entered Sebaian hidop, and is travelling towards Sebaian mati. If it enters Sebaian mati immediate death ensues, but in order to prevent this unfortunate conclusion, mannangs are employed to follow and overtake it while still in Sebaian hidop, and to bring it back to the body.

The Sebuyos believe that each man has seven semungats, and that sickness is caused by the loss of one of them. Very frequently also, illness is attributed to possession by an evil spirit, and sometimes to the presence of stones or other deleterious substances in the body.

But, whatever be the cause of sickness, the mannangs are considered able to cure it. When it is determined to invoke their aid, they assemble in the sick man's room, and there commence their dreary and monotonous chant, which it is so irksome to be compelled to listen to. It is frequently interrupted to allow them to partake of siri and betel-nut, and is again continued as dreary and as dismal as ever. After a while each mannang is furnished with a long bamboo filled with boiled rice, into which as into a scabbard he inserts his staff, and thus bears it about with him. Large heaped-up dishes of raw rice, each with an egg on the top, are placed in a line from the door of the room to the platform outside the house, and thither the mannangs walk in procession, each of them carefully treading in the dishes of rice. Their leader places his feet upon the eggs which are forced into the rice without breaking, the grain, like sand, receiving and sustaining the weight of the footsteps. Thus they arrive at the platform, where a space of 12 feet square has been fenced off for their reception. In the centre of this space a sort of conoidal pillar is erected and covered with red cloth, round which the mannangs perambulate in procession, uttering their dreary chant, and beating time with their rice-immersed staves. After a little time each is furnished with a small dish of parched rice, dyed rice, sugar and sago, or some other sweetmeat, holding which in their hands together with their staves, they continue their perambulation, and scatter the contents of their dishes as offerings to the spirits. Dishes and staves are now laid aside, and the young fruit branches of the betel-nut (which somewhat resemble broom besoms, only that they are of a pale straw-colour, and are covered with hundreds of embryo nuts) are produced and distributed to the performers. Holding these in their hands, they continue their walk, lifting them slowly above their heads as they move along, and bringing them down gently upon the floor. These motions, which are at first slow, become gradually quicker, and the mannangs soon break from the procession in which they have hitherto moved, all order amongst them is lost, they rush about and jostle each other in the confined space within which they are penned, still continuing to raise their pinang branches and to

strike the floor with them, until, breathless with their exertions,
they drop exhausted and pretend to swoon. This part of the ceremony affords great sport to the spectators, for as some of the
mannangs are generally blind, some striking collisions frequently
take place, and are hailed with a laughter which is grimly partici-
pated in by the performers themselves. As each drops he generally contrives to cover himself with his sarong, and thus they all
lie still and silent for about ten minutes. At length one of them
(they have probably agreed beforehand which of them it should
be) is seen to tremble all over. "He is now entering Sebaian."
Presently he is seen as it were to receive something, which he puts
into his girdle. "That is medicine which he gets from the
hantus." "Is it for the sick person?" "No." "What is it for?"
"He keeps it." "Does he do nothing with it?" "Another time
perhaps he gives it to some one else that is sick." Soon after receiving the medicine the tremour ceases, and he gets up, but he
never tells if he has seen the wandering soul, or has prevailed on it
to return to its earthly tenement. The rest rise about the same
time, and the ceremony is concluded. During the whole time a
hideous noise is kept up by beating gongs and drums, a mode of
procedure which, however unlikely to bring back a wandering soul,
may well be supposed capable of driving away every evil spirit that
possesses a sensitive tympanum.

In cases of possession by a hantu the mannangs assemble as
before in the sick man's room, which has been partially darkened
for the purpose, and after the usual amount of chanting and siri-
eating, a fowl is produced and sacrificed. By means of powerful
spells the evil spirit is compelled to quit his victim, and as he
passes through the doorway, which is left open on purpose, he is
seen by one of the mannangs (generally a blind one), who cuts at
him with a parang, and with such effect that blood is invariably
drawn, and is found scattered about the room.

Fish bones and stones are also said to be extracted from the
bodies of patients by the magically hooked fingers of the mannangs.
There are no peculiar symptoms by which their presence can be
detected, nor any theory by which it can be explained; nevertheless
the mannangs pretend to extract them from the inmost vitals of the
sick.

These superstitions are held almost universally, at least I have
heard only one person who professed to discredit them, a
youth named Nyambang, the most intelligent of the Balow Christians.
"The mannangs say," said he, "that they enter Sebaian, and see the
spirits; but how can they? They only pretend. They say that
they cut at the spirits and draw blood from them, but they do
it in the dark where no one can see, and it is fowl's blood they
sprinkle about. They say they draw fish bones and stones out of
men's bodies, but they don't; they conceal them between their
fingers in this manner (shewing how), and fumble about the sick

man's clothes, and then shew the bones and say they have drawn them out of his body. But it is all a lie, and they just want to get money. If I were sick, I would die sooner than be ber-man-nanged." He ridiculed with some humour and much contempt the proceedings of the mannangs in their various rites, much to the awe and somewhat to the horror of the surrounding youths, who evidently regarded him as broaching opinions bordering on the sacriligious. Sentiments such as these, however, are rare, and I doubt if there be another Dyak in the Rajah's territory who would endorse them.

Mannangs also assist at marriage rejoicings for the sake of good luck, but do not take any part in the ceremony. The Dyak phrase for to marry is to split a pinang, and the rite consists in a betel-nut being split in two, with certain formalities, and one part given to be eaten by the bride, the other by the bridegroom.

They have likewise a ceremony somewhat analogous to purification after childbirth. A portion of the platform is fenced off, in the centre of which the mother, holding the child in her arms, takes her seat. A female attendant shades her with an umbrella, and the mannangs walk round her chanting, beating time with their staves, and making offerings, till at a certain stage of the proceedings two of them lift her up, together with the stool on which she sits, while the rest continue their chant around her.

The Sarawak Dyaks burn, but the Balos, Sebuyos, Serebas, and Sakarrans, bury their dead. Among the latter the corpse, wrapped up in grave-clothes and laid on a bier, is towed in a canoe as near as possible to the burial ground, whether it is then carried by the attendants. The grave is then dug; articles of value are some-times buried along with the body, and the whole is made as secure possible. As soon after the funeral as an enemy's head has been taken (which now may not be for several years), the surviving relatives prepare to make at the tomb offerings of siri pinang, fruit cakes, and various other articles of food, together with beautiful miniature imitations in platted and coloured straw of almost all the articles of Dyak dress and furniture. These offerings are taken to the tomb and left there, the spirits being at the same time invoked with appropriate rites.

I once visited a Dyak burial place, and found it to be a very im-perfectly cleared piece of jungle on the side of a small hill at some distance from the houses. Among the graves were the bodies of some of their chiefs, placed in rude coffins and raised on stages some eight or ten feet high, similar to those of which I have read among the South Sea Islanders. Some of these relics of mortality were perceptibly recent; upon others nature had thrown the green mantle with which, in that country, she so soon obliterates all the untended works and traces of man. One of the bodies thus honoured was that of a woman, "a wise woman who knew all about planting paddy," and had thus earned a place in the Dyak Westminster.

All honour to the brave and the wise in their generation, to those who by their courage or talents have raised themselves above their fellowmen, however low the level from which they stand out. All honour to them, for they have gained a title to be held in remembrance by those they have left behind—a title which will be looked on with respect by every good man and true, in the brotherhood of nations. All honour to them again though their skins be brown and their dress scanty.

CHAPTER IV.

SOCIAL LIFE.

In every condition of existence, however low it may appear, man has been found to possess not merely the necessaries, but also some of the luxuries of life; not merely food to support his physical frame, but also stimulants agreeably to excite his nervous system. The Dyaks form no exception to this rule, and the stimulants which they employ are Tuak and Siri.

Tuak is a sort of unbittered beer made from rice, of greenish tinge and very capable of producing intoxication. It is prepared in great quantities previous to every feast, but it is not a general drink. It is dispensed with great liberality at many of their rejoicings, where it is considered a point of honour to send away the guests intoxicated, in so much that if any of them seems to resist its influence, the prettiest damsels of the house fasten upon him and ply him with cups till he yields to the power of the liquor.

The ordinary stimulant however is Siri, a pungent aromatic creeper, cultivated by the Dyaks for the sake of its leaves, which they thus use. A portion of a leaf is covered with lime, and in it a piece of betel-nut, a little tobacco, and some gambier (either the gum itself or the leaf) are rolled up, forming a quid which is chewed. It has a pungent astringent taste, colours the saliva red, and, if persevered in, dyes the teeth black. Its use is universal among the Dyaks, to whom it supplies the place of cake and wine, cigars and snuff, a pot of beer, or a cup of tea. It is produced at births, marriages, and deaths, in all assemblies, warlike, political, and judicial, at all feasts of rejoicing, and at all incantations for sickness; it is the universal cheerer and restorative, the all-healing medicine, and, when well chewed, the all-curing plaster. In every circumstance of life, fighting or trading, sick or well, travelling or staying at home, working or idling, sad, happy, or listless, the Dyak turns to his beloved Siri to cheer, to sooth, or to arouse him, and a physiologist will perhaps say that his simple food demands some such stimulant.

D

Siri and betel-nut are produced in great abundance in the country, and a coarse tobacco is likewise grown by the Dyaks of the interior. Those who live near the sea coast, however, chiefly purchase that which has been imported from Java or China, which being better cured, as well as of finer quality than their own, is likewise in great request among the tribes in the interior. Besides being eaten with siri, tobacco is also rolled into cigarettes and smoked. Gambier is grown in the country, and lime procured from oyster shells.

The custom by which the Dyaks are best known is that of cutting off and preserving the heads of their enemies, a barbarous method of perpetuating the memory of their exploit, which they celebrate with every sign of triumphant rejoicing. When a head has been taken, the brains are removed, and the eyeballs punctured with a parang, so as to allow their fluid contents to escape. If the boat in which the fortunate captor sails is one of a large fleet, no demonstrations of success are made, lest the head should excite the cupidity of some chief; but if she has gone out alone, or accompanied only by a few others, she is decorated with the young leaves of the nipa palm. These leaves, when unopened, are of a pale straw colour, and, when cut, their leaflets are separated and tied in bunches on numerous poles, which are stuck up all over the boat. At a little distance, they present the appearance of gigantic heads of corn projecting above the awning of the boat, and amongst them numerous gay-coloured flags and streamers wave in the breeze. Thus adorned, the boat returns in triumph; and the yells of her crew, and the beating of their gongs, inform each friendly house they pass of the successful result of their foray. The din is redoubled as they approach their own house. The shouts are taken up and repeated on shore. The excitement spreads; the shrill yells of the women mingle with the hoarser cries of the men, the gongs in the house respond to those in the boat, and all hurry to the wharf to greet the victors. Then there is the buzz of meeting, the eager question, the boastful answer, the shout, the laugh, the pride of triumph; and the gallant warriors become the cynosure of every eye—the envy of their equals, the admiration of the fair. When the excitement has in some degree subsided, the crew, leaving some of their number in the boat, go up to the house, where a plentiful supply of siri, pinang, and tobacco are produced, and over these Dyak cheerers of the social hour, the event is related and discussed in all its breadth and bearings. At length they prepare to bring the trophy to the house. A long bamboo is procured, and its lower joint split into several pieces, which are then opened out and wrought by means of rattans into a sort of basket. Into this basket the head is put, and is carried by the chief man in the boat from the wharf to the house, in the doorway of which, and at the head of the ladder, the principal woman of the house stands to receive it. The bearer, standing below, presents it to her, and as she endeavours to take it, withdraws it : he again presents and again withdraws it, till, at the seventh time, he allows her to obtain it. Thence she carries it to the bundle of skulls which hang in the open gallery, and it is there deposited along with the rest. As night approaches, preparations are made for drying, or rather roasting it. A fire is lighted in a little shed outside the house ; the head is suspended close above the flames ; and when it has been dried to satisfaction —that is, well smoked, and partially scorched—it is taken back and redeposited in the bundle, to remain there till it is feasted. "And what becomes of the flesh ?" I asked of an aged warrior, who was displaying to me a recently captured head, to which the scorched and shrivelled integuments still adhered, while from the earlier skulls all trace of flesh had long since disappeared. With the utmost nonchalance the old savage replied :—"The rats eat it."

In the meantime, friends, chiefly the young of both sexes, resort to the house to congratulate the successful warriors. Siri and pinang, the never-failing accompaniments of a Dyak meeting, are produced in great quantities ; the gongs and drums are beaten throughout the whole night ; and the victors, amid scenes of gaiety and sport,'rejoice in the admiring envy of the youths, and bask in the smiles of the fair. During the few succeeding days, feasting proceeds to a certain extent, and a basket of offerings to the spirits is suspended on the top of the house ; but the grand entertainment is delayed till an abundant harvest should enable them to celebrate the head-feast in a manner suited to the dignity of the occasion.

For this important event, which frequently does not take place for two or three years after the head has been taken, preparations are made some weeks previously. Large stores of cakes and sweetmeats are provided, and many jars of tuak, or native beer, are prepared ; much siri, pinang, and tobacco collected, and every preparation made for an extensive display of hospitality. On the morning of the appointed day, the guests, dressed in their best, and ornamented with all their barbaric finery, begin to assemble, and rarely, except on such occasions as these, are their savage ornaments now seen. Such at least, is the case among the Balos, a tribe who are in a sort of transition state between ancient barbarism and modern civilisation, and whose young men would now on ordinary occasions be ashamed to appear in those fantastic ornaments, which a few years ago were the delight of their hearts. I cannot say they have gained much in appearance by the change. A handsome savage, in his embroidered chawat, with his pure white armlets shining on his dusky arms, his brass-wire bracelets, his variegated head-dress of blue, white, and red, hung with shells, or adorned with the crimsoned hair of his enemies, and surmounted by the feathers of the argus pheasant, or by some artificial plume of his own invention, girt with his ornamented sword, and bearing in his hand a tall spear, as with free step he treads his native wilds, is a sight worthy of a painter. The same individual, clothed in a pair of dirty ragged trousers, with perhaps a venerable and well-worn shooting-jacket, the gift of some liberal European, suggests ideas of anything but the picturesque or the beautiful. Many of them, however, have adopted the Malay costume, which is both civilised and becoming, and have thereby effected a compromise between beauty and propriety.

But whatever costume they adopt, whether Dyak, Malay, or pseudo-European, all are clothed in the best garments they can procure; and they come in troops from the neighbouring houses to that in which the feast is to be held. As they arrive, eight or ten young men, each with a cup and a vessel of tuak, place themselves in a line inwards from the doorway, and as the company enter, they are presented by each of the tuak-bearers with a cup of the liquid. To drink is compulsory, and thus they all run the gauntlet of all the cups. As tuak is not a pleasant liquor to take in excess—the headache from it is tremendous—it is to the majority of them a penance rather than a pleasure, and many attempt but in vain, to escape the infliction. In this manner the male guests assemble and seat themselves in the gallery, the chiefs being conducted to the place of honour in the middle of the building, and beneath the bundle of skulls. All the rooms are at the same time thrown open, and each family keeps free house for the entertainment of the female guests. These as they arrive, enter and partake of the dainties that are provided for them; and many of the men being likewise invited to join them, the feast of reason and the flow of soul proceed as triumphantly as in similar cases in Europe. Cakes, sweetmeats, eggs, and fruit are produced, discussed, and washed down with tuak, and occasionally with a little arrack; while siri, pinang, gambier, and tobacco serve as devilled biscuits, to give zest and pungency to the substantial dessert. Conversation never for an instant flags; the laugh, the joke, the endless chatter, the broad banter, and the quick reply, pass unceasingly round the circle, and a glorious Babel of tongues astounds the visitor. Outside, in the gallery, the same scene is enacted, but with less animation than in the rooms, for, as there, the ladies form no part of the company—the assembly wants all its soul, and much of its life. The girls of the house, however, dressed in their gayest, and looking their best—"beautiful as stars," a Dyak once told me—have formed themselves into a corps of waitresses, and hand round the viands to the assembled guests. As it is not according to Dyak etiquette to take a thing when first offered, the young ladies have it very much in their own power as to who shall be helped, and to what extent—a privilege which, I have been told, they are inclined to exercise with great partiality. Poor Bonduk! never shall I forget thy disappointed mien, as, with dejected looks and downcast air, thou leantest against an adjacent doorway, mingling neither with the crowd within nor with those without, most sad and most forlorn amidst all the gaiety and racket.

"Well, Bondak," I said, for I liked the boy, "what is it? Are you not enjoying yourself?"

"It is nothing, sir," he answered, in melancholy tones; and then gathering courage, he thus poured forth his lugubrious complaint into what he deemed sympathising ears:—"The girls of this house are not liberal, sir; they don't give any cakes to boys like me (he was about fifteen); they give them all to the bachelors."

"Eh?" I uttered, in amazement.

"They give all the cakes and sweetmeats, and everything, to the bachelors; and they give some to the old men and little children; but they don't give any to boys like me."

I could not help smiling; but I thought it a hard case—hard that boys should be kept looking wistfully on while their seniors were eating cakes and sweetmeats. Accordingly, entering another room, I there accepted at once all that was offered me, and bringing it out, I gave it to Bondak, who shared it with his companions, and was happy.

The mamnangs, male and female, next take part in the ceremony. They congregate in the gallery, and seating themselves in a circle, one of them begins his dreary and monotonous chant, while the rest at stated intervals join in the chorus. They occasionally intermit their rhyme, in order to take a little refreshment; after which, another of the brotherhood takes the lead, and they continue their dismal monotone as before. After some time, each of them is furnished with a small plate of raw rice, dyed a bright saffron colour, holding which in their hands, they perambulate the crowded gallery, and, still continuing their chant, scatter the yellow grains over the seated multitude, "for luck."

In the meantime, the object of all this rejoicing, the captured head, hangs along with its fellow in the bundle almost unnoticed. In the morning, before any of the guests have assembled, some one has stuffed a half-rotten plantain into one eye, and fastened a piece of cake and a little siri and pinang near (not into) its mouth. It is then replaced in the bundle, and no more notice taken of it throughout the whole feast, unless a few boys, warriors in embryo, occasionally advance to inspect it. [It has been said by former writers that it is stuck upon a pole, and its mouth filled with choice morsels of food, but I never saw this done, nor did any Dyak whom I have questioned know anything of such a custom. As to the opinion that they endeavour to propitiate the souls of the slain, and get them to persuade their relatives to be killed also, or that the courage of the slain is transferred to the slayer—I am inclined to think that these are ideas devised by Malays, for the satisfaction of inquiring whites, who, as they would not be satisfied till they had reasons for everything they saw, got them specially invented for their own use.]

Offerings, however, are made to the superior powers. A pig has been killed early in the morning, and its entrails inspected to furnish

omens, while its carcase afterwards serves as materials for a feast.
Baskets of food and siri are hung up as offerings to the spirits and
to the birds of omen; among which latter, the burong *Penyala*, or
rhinoceros hornbill, is reckoned especially the bird of the spirits.
The grand event of the day, however, is the erection of lofty poles,
each surmounted by a wooden figure of the burong Penyala, which
is placed there "to peck at their foes." These figures are rather
conventional representations than imitations of nature, and do not
convey a very exact idea of the bird they are intended to represent.
Still they so far resemble the original, as to possess a body, head,
and tail; and they have likewise a long slender bill, and a horn
twisted like an ammonite. They are about twenty inches long,
painted in an astonishingly variegated manner, after the most
approved Dyak fashion, the heads being often decorated with a
downy crest. They are made some time previous to the festival,
and a day or two before it are carried about to the different houses
in the vicinity, accompanied by gongs and flags, to levy contri-
butions for the benefit of the feast. The poles on which they are
to be elevated are young trees, some of them about forty-five
inches in circumference at the lower end, and eighty feet in length;
posts so long and so heavy, that it may well be matter of surprise how men, unaided by ropes and pulleys, could erect them.
The method employed, however, is both simple and effective; the
posts are carried up, and laid on the platform of the house, and
two frameworks, about twenty feet high, and thirty feet long,
are erected parrallel to, and within a yard of each other, on the
ground at the end of the platform. These are constructed some
days previously, and are so placed that the lower end of the post,
when launched off the platform, may pass between them. When
it is intended to erect the post, the burong Penyala, together with
a proper amount of flags and streamers, is fixed on its upper end;
and it is then pushed along the platform till its lower end, projecting beyond it, and passing between the frameworks, is over-
balanced by its own weight, and falls to the ground. The post
then lies at an angle of about twenty degrees to the horizon, one end
resting on the ground, while its middle is supported by the platform. One of the Dyaks below then advances with a fowl in one
hand, and a drawn parang in the other; and placing the neck of
the bird upon the end of the post, chops its head off, and smears
the base of the post with its blood. After this sacrificial ceremony,
the signal for raising it is given. The Dyaks swarm upon the
two frameworks before mentioned, and putting their shoulders
under the post, while its lower end is kept fixed upon the ground,
they mount up by degrees to the top of the framework, and thus
gradually elevate it. The beak of the Penyala is then pointed in
the direction of the foe whom they wish it to peck at; and the
mast-like pole, securely lashed to the two frameworks, stands at
once a trophy of victory and a symbol of defiance. Eight or ten

such posts are erected, a fowl being sacrificed on each ; and about half-way up the largest, which is erected first, a basket of fruit, cakes, and siri is suspended, as an offering to the spirits.

Meanwhile, those who remain in the house still continue the feast, and those who have been engaged in erecting the posts return to it as soon as their labour is finished. The festivities are prolonged far on into the night, and they are resumed and continued, though with abated vigour, during the two following days.]

The poles, in the preparation and erection of which so much labour is expended, are permitted to remain for about a fort-night, after which they are taken down, and the Penyala given to the children ; new ones being generally made for each festivity.*

The head-feast is the greatest of their feasts ; the next in impor-tance is what we would call a house-warming, or what they denominate a house-washing ; that is, the entertainment given in honour of a new house. As soon as the first harvest after its erection has given the community a plentiful supply of paddy, preparations for it similar to those made for the head-feast, but on a much less extensive scale, are commenced ; but as the rejoicings on this occasion always begin with cock-fighting—a sport which we discountenanced as much as possible, and of course never went near—I never witnessed them till the afternoon. By this time most of the guests had departed ; the majority of those who remained were lying about in a pitiable state of intoxication, while the rest, with red eyes, staggering gait, and wretched attempts at finery, were forming a procession round a few decorated pillars in the house, chanting and beating time with their staves like mannangs. It was a miserable sight, and not such as to tempt me to go back ; consequently, though I had many subse-quent opportunities of witnessing the whole affair, I never again went near it.

Drunkenness, however, is not a vice to which the Dyaks are much addicted. True, they will take arrack when it is offered them ; and there are certain times when they consider it a duty to become intoxicated, or at least to intoxicate their guests ; but they are not habitually drunken, and no Dyak would spend his money upon liquor. They are too sensible of its value, and of the proba-bility of their being compelled to purchase rice with it before next harvest, thus to waste it. Much less would they think of parting with any of their property, their gongs, or jars, merely for the pur-pose of acquiring such a temporary gratification. In fact they are a remarkably acquisitive and accumulative people, and now that their constant fighting is put a stop to, and the destruction of each other's property thus prevented, I think it very likely that many of them may rise to considerable wealth ; and that they may ulti-

* The Dyaks say that if a man, when running, is cleverly decapitated by a stroke of a parang, the body will continue to run while the head is rolling on the ground.

mately become a more important social body even than the Malays. The life of a Malay is a succession of expedients. If he can meet a temporary want by a temporary contrivance he is satisfied, and contentedly allows each day to bring its own necessities and its own supplies. But it is not so with the Dyaks; they are much more provident, and seldom hesitate to undertake a little present trouble for the sake of a future reward.

CHAPTER V.

ARTS OF LIFE.

There are many different languages spoken by the various tribes of Dyaks, all of which, from their resemblance to Malay and to each other, may be grouped together as languages of the Malay family. The resemblance borne to Malay by the language of the Balos (which is the same as that of the Sebuyos, Sakarrans, and various other tribes) is very considerable, but it appears to proceed from their being both originally derived from a common source, rather than from one of them being an offshoot of the other. The Balo language is much more complex and much more difficult than Malay, is very copious and exceedingly idiomatic, is characterised by a great abundance of specific and great absence of generic terms, has names for articles which the Dyaks no longer possess, and presents many other marks of being the language of a people who have retrograded in civilization.

That the Dyaks were at one time more civilized than they are at present is a conclusion which may likewise be drawn from the existence among them of many of the arts of life—arts which seem to belong to a higher type of civilization than they at present exhibit, and which appear to be the happily preserved wrecks of that higher civilization from which they have now degenerated. Many things point to India as the source of this civilization. Stone bulls and sacrificing stones, exactly similar to those now used in India, are found in Borneo, although not now used by the natives for any religious purpose; while many of the arts of life, those especially in which their comparative superiority is most strongly marked, are exactly the same as those of India. I think, therefore, it may be safely assumed that an intimate connection between Hindostan and Borneo formerly existed, perhaps while the aborigines of the former country (who may have been of the same race with the Dyaks*) were its exclusive possessors; and during this period the civilization of Borneo was, I have no doubt, comparatively high. Isolation from India, however—caused, probably, by the conquest of that country by the Hindoos, together with the barbarism induced by incessant internal wars—have gradually reduced the Dyaks to the state in which they now are, and thus they add another to the many examples which history affords of the instability of all civilization which is not based upon true religion.

Egypt, Assyria, Babylon, Persia, Greece, and Rome, all have flourished and decayed, and the decay of each can, I think, be traced to their false religions. So long as the people believed their mythology—so long as they believed in the existence of Deities who saw, and judged, and rewarded, and punished men according to their deeds—they had a constraining power upon their conscience not greatly different from that of the Christian, and while they held this belief they were to a great extent virtuous, industrious, energetic, and progressive. As soon, however, as the progress of civilization had taught them the absurdity of their own religion, they lost belief in it, without acquiring any other, and thus their modes of thought became entirely governed by objects of sense. Hence it followed that the manners of the nation became corrupt, and its intellect deadened, and it retrograded as surely as it had formerly progressed. Thus has it been in all past history, and thus will it be in all time to come. As surely as the religious life of a nation becomes extinct, so surely is its national life near its end; and as there is but one religion which will bear the most thorough investigation from the most profound, acute, and subtle intellects, so it is that religion, and that religion alone, which is fitted to conduct man to the highest and most permanent type of civilization.

Though the Dyaks are a mild and gentle people, they carry on their wars with the most ruthless barbarity. I have often felt it passing strange when, after playing with a number of quiet, gentle, girlish-looking boys, I have sat down beside them in the cool of the evening, and listened to them telling, with the utmost unconcern, and as a mere matter of course, stories of the most revolting and blood-thirsty cruelty, some of which they had themselves witnessed, and all of which they were evidently prepared to see re-enacted to-morrow without compunction and without surprise. Still, ruthless and barbarous as the Dyaks are in their wars, they are not without a touch of chivalry. The Kanowit Dyaks having been accustomed, like the Sarebas and Sakarrans, to go out on piratical expeditions, a fort was built at the mouth of their river in

---

* It may be objected that no trace of a Malay or Mongolian race (I regard the two as substantially the same) is to be found in the plains of India. We must remember, however, that the Turks—originally a Mongolian race—present now all the features of the Caucasian; and that the Pitcairn Islanders—all of whose mothers, and many of whose fathers, were Malayo-Polynesians—also, I believe, exhibit exclusively the characteristics of Caucasians. It may well be, then, that a Mongolian type has disappeared from India, through intermarriage of the Mongolian race with their Caucasian conquerors.

E

order to stop them; but, although a few of the tribe agreed to give up this practice, and settled in the vicinity of the fort, the majority, under the chieftainship of Buah Ryah, refused to do so. The consequence was that the fleets of Buah Ryah, in their attempts to pass the fort, had many collisions with the garrison; and the two parties—the followers of Buah Ryah and the subjects of the Rajah—regarded each other as enemies whose heads it was laudable and proper to take by all possible means. On one occasion, one of the Malay fortmen having lost himself in the jungle, wandered about for two days till, on the second night, he came by chance to the house of one of the followers of Buah Ryah. He boldly entered, told the inmates who he was, and said they might take his head if they liked, but added that he hoped they would give him some food first, as he had had nothing to eat for two days. Some rice was produced, and, while he was eating it, conversation turned upon the last fight that had taken place between Buah Ryah and the fort, and the various devices which each party had adopted, or intended to adopt. Being unwilling, however, to trust himself to the generosity of his new-made friends longer than he was compelled to do so, he left the house immediately after he had finished his meal, and, saying that he would soon be back, made towards the wharf, took one of the canoes that was lying there, and was soon paddling down the stream on his way to the fort, which he reached in safety.

The ordinary boats of the Dyaks are long, narrow canoes, hollowed out of the trunk of a tree, the sides being raised by planks pinned upon them. Their war-boats, however, are much larger, and are constructed differently. The lunas, or keel plank, which is of the entire length of the boat, has two ledges on its inside, each of them about an inch from each margin of the plank. Each of the other planks, which are likewise the entire length of the boat, has an inside ledge on its upper margin, its lower margin being plain, like an ordinary plank. When the Dyaks have made as many planks as are necessary for the boat they intend constructing, they put them together in the following manner:—The lunas, or keel plank, being properly laid down, the first side plank is brought and placed, with its lower or plain edge, upon the ledge of the keel-plank. The ledge of the first side-plank being thus uppermost, it becomes in turn the ledge upon which the lower edge of the second side-plank must rest. The ledges of the keel-plank, and of the first side-plank, are then pierced, and firm rattan lashings passed from the one to the other. The lower edge of the second side-plank is in like manner laid upon the ledge of the first, and these two planks are lashed together in the same way as the first was lashed to the keel. Thus they place the edge of each plank upon the ledge of that immediately below it, lashing them both firmly together; and when they have in this manner put on as many planks as they wish (generally four or five on each side), they caulk the seams, so as to render the boat water-tight. Hence, in the construction of their boats they not only employ no nails, treenails, or bolts, but even no timbers—nothing but planks ingeniously lashed together by rattans, and then caulked. It is true that these lashings are not very durable, as the rattans soon get rotten; but this is of little consequence, since, whenever a boat returns from an expedition, the lashings are cut, and the planks being separated, are taken up into the house. When she is again wanted, the planks are taken down, and the boat reconstructed as before. To propel their boats they employ paddles of about three feet in length—never oars, and seldom sails.

The facility with which their boats can be taken to pieces is sometimes of essential service to them. If they have come down their own river on a war expedition, and find on their return that a powerful force has assembled to prevent their re-ascending, they turn back and go up some other river, the tributaries of which pass near their own country. When they have in this manner come as near their own houses as they can, they draw their boats ashore, cut the lashings which hold them together, and five or six men, shouldering each of the planks, they carry the boat home piece-meal through the jungle.

The principal cutting instruments employed by the Dyaks in their wood work are parangs and biliongs. The parang is a thick, short, heavy sword, or rather chopping-knife, about two feet in length, and of which either the blade is curved like a Turkish scymitar, or if the blade be straight the handle is bent backward, so as to form an acute angle with it. The parang is employed in war as well as for more peaceful purposes, and in the jungle is indispensible, as without it the Dyak would find it impossible to make his way through the thickets which he is frequently obliged to penetrate. It is, moreover, applied to every purpose which a knife will serve, and is at once a warrior's blade, a woodman's bill, and a carpenter's tool-chest.

The biliong is a kind of axe constructed so that its cutting-edge may be placed either parallel or at right angles to its handle, in order to serve either for an axe or an adze, as circumstances may require. It is employed for cutting down trees, hewing out planks, and such other heavy work as the parang would be unfit for.

The above mentioned instruments are formed by the Dyaks from iron which they purchase from the Malays and Chinese, but there is another kind of chopping-knife or Ilang made by the Kyans, who not only forge but also smelt the iron of which it is formed. Unlike the parang, the cutting edge of the Ilang is straight, and is in the same straight line with its handle, while the blade is round on one side and flat on the other, somewhat like the blade of a pair of scissors. In consequence of this peculiarity of structure, Ilangs are adapted for cutting with one hand only, but they are sometimes made in pairs, one for each hand. They are very much prized by the Dyaks, and some of them are so beautiful that they would be no discredit to an English workman. Indeed, it seems marvellous, and almost incredible, that such blades should be smelted, forged, and wrought by savages, or rather we ought to draw the conclusion that men who can produce such blades do not deserve such a degrading epithet.

The parang is equally an instrument of industry and a weapon of warfare; their other weapons are spears, shields, darts, and another peculiar to themselves called the sumpitan. Their spears are about seven or eight feet long, the head generally of iron (though I have seen them made of a hard kind of wood), and lashed to the shaft with split rattan. Their shields, which are made of wood or bark, are about four feet long and eighteen inches wide. They have one handle in the centre, and the front, which is curved, is painted and often ornamented with human hair. Their darts are simply pointed pieces of wood about four feet long, and to a European would not appear very effective, but they are made of such hard wood (the nibong, a kind of palm) that they are capable of receiving a very sharp point, and when thrown at a short distance would pierce a man. The sumpitan, or blow pipe, is a wooden tube of about eight feet in length and an inch in diameter, through which small poisoned arrows are blown with such effect that they are capable of wounding at the distance of thirty yards. The arrow is a small splinter of nibong about as thick as a stocking wire, stuck into a small hemispherical base of very light wood, so as to afford a surface for the breath to act upon. The point is cut sharp, and steeped in vegetable poison (a case of which they carry with them), and into which they again dip the arrow immediately before discharging it. These arrows the Dyks use in hunting as well as in war, and kill not only birds and squirrels with them, but also large animals such as orang-utans. To animals the poison proves fatal, because they cannot pull the arrow out of the wound; but men suffer little inconvenience from it, as their comrades can always extract the missile before the poison has been absorbed by the system. Squirrels and small animals drop a few minutes after they have been struck, but orang-utans frequently clamber about among the trees for a whole day before the poison takes such effect upon them as to bring them down. Sometimes the spear and the sumpitan are combined, a spear head being lashed upon the tube of the sumpitan, thus in some degree affording the advantages of a musket and bayonet.

The principal crop which the Dyaks grow is rice, and their agricultural operations are extremely simple. Having selected the piece of ground which they intend to farm, and which is invariably overgrown with jungle, their first care is to erect a farm-house in which to reside with their families during the season of cultivation. They then clear a few square yards of ground, which they sow thickly with rice, and while this is growing they continue to clear as much more as they think they will cultivate. When they have thus cut down the trees and bushes over as large a space as they intend to plant they set fire to it, its ashes forming an excellent manure, and then pulling up the rice which they formerly sowed they transplant it widely over the space which they have thus cleared. With some tribes the operation is still simpler. When the ground has been cleared and the brushwood burnt the Dyak, with a long pointed stick, dibbles a number of holes, into each of which his wife, who follows him, drops a few grains of rice, and then gives it a scratch with a stick so as to fill it up. While the crop is growing it receives considerable attention, is weeded and defended as much as possible from wild pigs, birds, and other destructive animals, and when it is ripe the heads of corn are cut off, brought home, and beaten out. After the harvest has been secured the ground is abandoned, and in the succeeding year they make their farms in another place. Thus they continually change their rice grounds year after year, till they return to the spot they originally cultivated, and thus instead of a rotation of crops they employ a rotation of fields. This they do for two reasons ; first, that the ground may lie fallow; and secondly, because immediately after the crop is reaped the ground is so covered with grass, reeds, shoots of young trees, and weeds of all sorts that the labour of clearing it then would be excessive. In the course of six or seven years, however, the young trees have shot up to such a height that they have suffocated the grass and other weeds beneath them, so that when the Dyaks return to this piece of ground in order to clear it, they have merely to cut down and burn the young trees, after which they resume their farming operations as before.

The animals which the Dyaks hunt are chiefly wild pigs and deer. The former are often taken in pitfalls, sometimes in a kind of trap so constructed as to spear them when they approach it ; but more frequently they are hunted with dogs ; the latter are generally snared in the following manner :—A long rattan rope with a great many nooses depending from it is stretched in the jungle, and the deer are driven into it by bands of men and dogs. The process of snaring is generally carried on at night, and from the number of men employed, each of whom is armed with sword and spear, their savage whoops and yells, mingled with the barking of the dogs, and ringing far and wide through the dark forest, presents a most exciting, and to a European, a somewhat awe-inspiring scene.

In fishing the Dyaks sometimes use hook and line, but more generally different kinds of nets. One of these exactly resembles the salmon nets of this country, only that it is constructed of bamboos and rattans instead of cords ; another, which can only be used for the capture of small fish in shallow water, is the casting net. This is a circular net of about twelve feet in diameter, its circumference being loaded with lead and so tied in that the diameter of the extreme margin is less than that of the net a few inches within it. When about to use it, the fisherman, standing in the bow of his canoe, holds it by the centre, allowing the loaded circumference to hang down, and when he has been paddled by his companion to a proper place he casts it so that the loaded circumference flies open, and drops upon the water in a circle. The weights attached to it carry it to the bottom, and all the fish within the circumference are thus enclosed. The fisherman, by then pulling the centre towards him, contracts the circumference, and as the extreme margin has been tied in so that its diameter is less than that of the net a few inches above it, the efforts of the fish to escape, being naturally made against the widest part of the net, are of course ineffectual. As the net thus becomes more and more contracted the fish become entangled in it, and when, by gradually lifting up the centre, the circumference has been drawn together, the net with its contents is lifted into the boat. The fish are then taken out, and the net prepared for another cast.

Another method of fishing is by wooden floats, generally of the form of a duck, each with a baited hook attached to it, and set swimming down the stream. The owner of these floats glides in his canoe among them, plying his rod and line, and watching till the peculiar motions of any of the ducks should shew that a fish has been hooked.

There is another method practised by the Malays for the capture of large fish as they ascend the rivers from the sea with the flood tide. Two lines of posts—one from each bank of the river—reach diagonally across half the channel, and meet in the centre in the former of the letter V, the apex lying up the stream. At the apex several long posts are driven deep into the bottom, and stand up high above the water, forming as it were the framework of a kind of watch-tower, in the water beneath which a net capable of being quickly raised to the surface is set. One man stationed below watches to see the fish enter, while the rest, stationed on the framework, man the tackle by which the net is to be hoisted up. The lines of posts before mentioned form leaders to bring the fish into the net, and as soon as the man on the outlook sees one within it he gives the signal to his companions, by whom net and fish are quickly raised out of the water.

Their most peculiar mode of fishing, however, is what is called tuba fishing, tuba being the root of a poisonous plant employed for the purpose of stupifying the fish, which are then speared. When a tuba fishing is determined on, fifty or a hundred boats collect, with perhaps 400 or 500 bundles of tuba, and, having selected the river which they intend to fish, they first make across it a barrier of stakes, with a receptacle in the centre to receive such of the fish as may be stupified but escape being speared. They then go several miles higher up the stream, and, having taken a quantity of water into their boats, they begin to beat the tuba amongst it. Thus they mingle its juice with the water in the canoe, forming thereby a dirty white-looking fluid, which they throw into the river, and which, mingling with the stream, stupifies all the fish with which it comes in contact. These as they rise to the surface are leistered by the Dyaks, while such as escape this fate are drifted down by the current into the receptacle before formed, and are there secured. It may easily be imagined that tuba fishing is a most interesting and exciting sport, and as it often takes place at night by torchlight the multitude of boats floating about on the dark river, each with its torches, throwing into strong relief the dusky and nearly naked figures of the crew, and partially lighting up the distant gloom of the forest, the glancing of the paddles, the hushed motions of the rowers, the erect figure of the spearsman with his three-pronged spear, as the little canoes float over the dark river and beneath the high over-arching trees, or dash on with foaming speed amid the yells of the crew, and urged by the contending efforts of rivals to the capture of some large fish, dimly seen struggling at a distance, form a singular and interesting spectacle.

Besides farming, fishing, and hunting, the principal employment of the Dyaks is collecting the produce of the jungle, the chief of which are gutta percha, katio and mengkabang oils, bees' wax, and edible birds' nests. Gutta percha (literally gum of Sumatra) is the sap of a forest tree, and is so well known that I need not describe it. It is procured by cutting down the tree and then chopping the bark throughout the whole length of the trunk, so as to allow the sap to ooze out. This it does in such quantities that it drops upon large leaves which the Dyaks have placed to receive it, whence it is collected into balls or cakes, and is ready for the market. India-rubber likewise is obtained from a creeping plant, but is scarcely as yet an article of commerce.

Mengkabang, or vegetable tallow, is procured in the following manner from one of the wild fruits of the jungle :—When the fruit, a species of nut, has been gathered, it is picked, dried, and pounded, and after being thoroughly heated in a shallow cauldron, it is put into a rattan bag and subjected to a powerful pressure. The oil oozes from the bag, and being run into bamboo moulds is there allowed to cool, in which state it becomes hard and yellow, somewhat resembling unpurified bees' wax. It is principally used by the Dyaks and Malays for cooking, being very palatable, but in this country it is employed for the manufacture of patent candles, for which it is superior to palm oil.

Katio oil is procured from another wild nut, and is expressed in a somewhat similar manner. It is a beautiful yellow transparent fluid, with a smell very much like bitter almonds, and I have little doubt that it will yet be found a very valuable article of commerce.

The press employed by the Dyaks in expressing these oils is, like many other of their contrivances, both simple and effective. It consists of two semi-cylindrical logs about 7 feet long, placed in an upright position, their flat surfaces being fitted together and their lower ends securely fastened to each other. On each of their upper ends a stout nob is cut, and a third piece of wood, about two feet long, nine inches wide, and two inches thick, with a hole cut in it about a foot long and three inches wide, is put over the nobs so as to clasp them together. Wedges are then inserted between the outside of the nob and the inside of the hole, and these when driven home subject whatever is between the logs to a powerful pressure.

The chief difficulty in collecting the above oils arises from the singular fact, that the nuts from which they are extracted are one year produced in great abundance, and the next in very small quantities. This uncertainty of crop is not confined to these two nuts, but extends to every fruit in the country, and singular as it may appear, every third year seems to be the year of overflowing abundance, while the two succeeding years are years of comparative scarcity. Fruit alone seems liable to this periodical increase and failure, at least I have never heard of it in reference to grain or other crops.

The wild bees which yield honey and wax build their nests only upon the tapang tree, one of the loftiest in the jungle; from the branches of each of this species several clusters are generally seen depending at a time. [Though situated in the heart of the jungle these trees are the property of individuals, and descend from father to son like any other possession, conferring upon their owner a right to the honey and wax they may yield.] When the Dyaks intend to appropriate the luscious produce, they assemble by night at the foot of the tapang tree which they wish to despoil, and one of them taking with him a light, a basket, and the end of a long rattan rope, ascends the trunk by means of little pegs driven into it. [When he has arrived at the branch from which the comb hangs he puts over it the end of the rope which he has brought with him, to which he forthwith attaches the basket, and cautiously slips the bight of of the rope along the bough till the basket hangs directly under the comb. He then with his parang loosens the comb so as to allow it to drop into the basket, and giving the signal to his companions (who hold the other end of the rope), comb and basket are quickly lowered to the ground. In the meantime he must defend himself with his light from the attacks of the bees in the best manner he can, and he wisely makes a speedy descent. When engaged in robbing a bees' nest the Dyak encumbers himself with as little clothing as possible, saying that if a bee lights upon his skin he can easily brush it off, but if it gets inside his jacket or trousers " it is a hard matter."

Besides the bee which produces wax and honey there is another species somewhat resembling the humble bee, but smaller, which forms its comb not of wax but of resin.

The edible bird's nest so prized by the Epicures of China is formed by a species of swallow which builds in the recesses of mountain caves. These caves, like the tapang trees, are the property of certain tribes, and before the Government of Rajah Brooke was established bloody fights for their possession frequently took place. Nests are of three qualities—Nos. 1, 2, and 3. No. 1 is composed entirely of a gelatinous-looking substance which breaks with a shining fracture, and when allowed to stand in water becomes soft and transparent; No. 2 is composed of the same substance, intermixed with feathers; while No. 3, which is somewhat like a blackbird's nest, consists of mud and grass, with considerable portions of gelatinous substance interspersed. Nos. 1 and 2 are attached to the sides of the cave in which they are found much as a swallow's nest is attached to the corner of a window in England; while No. 3, which I have only seen in China and not at all in Borneo, bears no marks of any such attachment, seeming to be merely placed on some receptacle like the nests of ordinary birds. The gelatinous substance of which they are composed is believed by the French naturalists to be a kind of sea-weed, but it is considered by Professor Owen to be an animal substance elaborated by the bird itself. It would be presumptuous in me to offer an opinion, but I may state that the caves in which these nests are found are at the distance of many days' journey from the sea, while I am not aware of a single place near the coast where they are to be obtained. The soup, which in itself is almost tasteless, may be seasoned to suit any palate, and is prized by the Chinese more for its invigorating qualities than for its flavour.

Except when employed in assisting in the operations of the farm, the time of the women is exclusively occupied in their household work, or in some branch of domestic industry, such as spinning, weaving, or mat-making. In sewing they prefer European needles and thread; but if they fail to obtain these they make use of those of their own manufacture. Their needles are of brass wire, one end being sharpened to a point, the other flattened and pierced for the eye. Their thread, which is of single twist, is spun upon a wheel which exactly resembles those employed in India; and their loom and method of weaving differ little, if at all, from those of the Hindoos. The cloth which they weave is of two kinds, striped and figured, the former for their jackets, the latter for their bidangs or petticoats. The former is made by employing successively threads of different colours in stretching the web; the latter is produced by a more difficult and elaborate process. After the web has been stretched (for which, in this case, undyed thread is employed) the work-woman sketches on the extended threads the pattern which she purposes shall appear on the cloth, and carefully notes the intended colours of the various scrolls. Supposing she intends the pattern to be of three colours, blue, red, and yellow, she proceeds as follows :—She takes up a dozen or a score of the threads of the web (according as the exigencies of the pattern will permit her) and wraps a quantity of vegetable fibre tightly round those parts of them which are intended to be red and yellow, leaving exposed those portions which are intended to be blue. After she has in this manner gone over the whole web, she immerses it in a blue dye, which, while it takes hold of the exposed portions of the threads, is prevented by the vegetable fibre from colouring those

F

portions which are intended to be red and yellow. After it has been dried the vegetable fibre is cut off; and when the web is now stretched out the blue portion of the pattern is seen depicted. In a similar manner the red and yellow colours are applied, and thus the whole web is dyed of the required pattern. The weft is of one uniform colour, generally brown.]

Embroidery is practised chiefly to ornament the ends of the men's chawats; and some of the patterns which they sew are very elaborate and rather pretty. There is, however, little variety in their designs, as they do not now seem able to originate new patterns; they only copy those which already exist, and which are lent from one to another for that purpose.

They make various kinds of mats, some for drying their grain upon, others to serve as beds and carpets. Some of the latter are very fine, and are much prized.

The principal food of the Dyaks is rice and salt, to which is occasionally added a little fish, venison or wild pig. When their rice is nearly finished, which it generally is just before harvest, they are compelled to resort to expedients to lengthen out their supplies. The Sarebas and Sakarran tribes plant Indian corn, which comes in opportunely at this time; an example which the Balos have begun to imitate, while some of the Sarawak tribes are able to procure a little sago from the few sago palms that are found in their vicinity. Many, however, are put to sad shifts, and are obliged to live upon fern tops and the shoots of such other plants as they collect in the jungle. There is a kind of clay which they sometimes resort to, and which I have seen eaten by boys from choice. It somewhat resembles pipeclay, but is streaked with red, probably the oxide of iron, and it appeared also to have a little chalk or some other salt of lime intermixed with it. It has a peculiar taste, which I could fancy might be liked by those accustomed to it, but it cannot contain much nourishment, and is only resorted to by adults as a last resource.

The chief condiment of the Dyaks is salt, which they procure from the nipa palm, and which they much prefer to that obtained by evaporation from sea water. The boughs of the nipa are cut, dried, and burnt, and their ashes washed in water, so as to dissolve the salt contained in them. This water being then allowed to run off clear is evaporated in pans, the salt remaining at the bottom of the vessel. It is a dirty grey and often black looking substance, possessing a slightly bitter taste, which is grateful to the palate of the Dyaks; and as it is generally produced in masses of considerable size and as hard as a stone, it has much the appearance of a mineral that has been dug out of the earth. Another product of the nipa is sugar, or rather treacle, which is manufactured from its fruit, and is very palatable. Vinegar is procured from another palm, by collecting its juice and allowing it to undergo the acetous fermentation, and from several others toddy is obtained: some kinds of which smell and taste strongly of sulphuretted hydrogen.

As soon as a Dyak acquires a little wealth, he invests it in the purchase of jars, brass swivels, or gongs. The jars, which they prize with a sort of superstitious reverence, are brown glazed earthenware, about three feet high, exactly the shape of Chinese jars, and many of them stamped with the Chinese imperial dragon. The Dyaks can give no account of their origin, but suppose them to be the work of Iuntus. The cost of the dragon jars is about 70 rls.; those not impressed with the dragon are called rusa, or deer jars, and are valued at about 30 rls., but there are others peculiarly sacred which fetch much higher prices, some of them being valued even at 800 rls. On one occasion, when a case involving one of these valuable jars was being tried in Sarawak, one of the European magistrates asking why it was prized so highly, received from one of the Malays the following answer:—" When God made the heavens there was some earth left over, and this jar was made of it." Such an answer, which in the present case was received with shouts of laughter by all present, is an instance of a reason fabricated for the occasion, for no such belief is entertained by the Dyaks.

Brass swivels, or lelas, are sold at so much per catty, as are likewise gongs, which latter are musical instruments, as well as representatives of wealth. Besides gongs, their principal musical instruments are drums, fiddles, and flutes. The drum is about four feet long, and six inches in diameter; one end, covered with pigs' skin, is beaten with the fingers, the other is left open for the passage of the sound. Their fiddles and flutes are so rude in construction, and so rarely used, that they are not worth describing.

The plants and animals of Sarawak are very much the same as those which have often been described as existing in other tropical islands, but there are some which to me were quite new, and which struck me as being so singular that I cannot forbear mentioning them—these are flying lizards, flying frogs, and creeping fish. The flying lizards have a pair of membranous wings, which they can expand or fold up at pleasure, and with which they can take long flying leaps from one tree to another. The flying frogs, which likewise live among trees (to the trunks and boughs of which their long claws enable them to adhere), have very large membranous paws and feet, with which they also take long flying leaps from tree to tree. The creeping fish, however, though by far the most common, are the most singular of all. They are about nine inches long, and are regular fish in all respects; their only peculiarities of form being the position of the eyes, which resemble two little balls placed on the top of the head, and the structure of their pectoral fins, which are fleshy and jointed, somewhat like the fore feet of a seal. They leave the water at pleasure, and come ashore in shoals upon the beach to feed, walking about by means of their pectoral fins, and dragging their bodies after them. Their pace when walking is very slow, but when alarmed they bound along the beach with great rapidity, making long leaps by means of their tails, bounding also, when they please, along the surface of the water like a ricochetting stone.

All these animals are, doubtless, well known to naturalists, but on one occasion there was brought me an animal which was not only very singular, but which I am inclined to regard as new. It was somewhat larger than a rat, to the head of which its head bore a striking resemblance, but it was four-handed, its habitat was evidently the branches of trees, and its general appearance much more resembled a monkey than any other animal. Its tail was bare, like that of a rat, but it had at the extremity a tuft of hair. Its fore paws, which were extremely short, it used like hands to convey its food to its mouth; it could climb like a monkey with great facility, but on level ground its progress was like that of the kangaroo, by a succession of leaps. It was very pugnacious, and sprung at any one who approached it with a sharp kind of bark. But, while its body so much resembled in detail those of the monkey, the rat, and the kangaroo, its motions, manners, and general appearance put one irresistibly in mind of a squirrel; so that, altogether, it is the most curious living mammal I ever saw. My first idea (derived from faint recollections of popular works on natural history), was that it was a jerboa, but it bears no resemblance to the jerboas in the British Museum. One of the officials of that institution, to whom I described it, shewed me an animal with a tuft at its tail, which had been sent home from Borneo; but it was not at all like that which I am endeavouring to describe. Indeed, I saw nothing in the Museum (except, perhaps, some of the smaller monkeys) which bore to it even a generic resemblance; and I have little doubt that it is a new animal. None of the Dyaks knew what it was, or had ever seen it before, so that it must be rare even in Sarawak. Unfortunately, it was killed, and partly devoured by rats during the night, and I never saw or heard of another specimen.

I have thus endeavoured to give an account of a country well known, by report at least, to the civilized world; and if I shall have succeeded in interesting any one in the people whom we have there been endeavouring, and with wonderful success, to Christianize, so as to induce them to lend a helping hand in the good work, I shall have fully realized the object I proposed in penning these sketches in Borneo. I am but too well aware of their imperfection; nevertheless, I trust they will be accepted, for, whatever they are in other respects, they have at least the merit of being faithful.

FINIS.